MILE END

To Arnaud

Copyright © 2019 by Isabelle Arsenault

All rights reserved. Published in the United States by Random House Children's Books,
a division of Penguin Random House LLC, New York. Published simultaneously in Canada
by Tundra Books, Toronto, in 2019.

Random House and the colophon are registered trademarks of Penguin Random House LLC.

Visit us on the Web! rhcbooks.com

Educators and librarians, for a variety of teaching tools, visit us at RHTeachersLibrarians.com

Library of Congress Cataloging-in-Publication Data is available upon request.

ISBN 978-0-553-53656-0 (trade) — ISBN 978-0-553-53657-7 (lib. bdg.) —
ISBN 978-0-553-53658-4 (ebook)

MANUFACTURED IN CHINA
10 9 8 7 6 5 4 3 2 1
First American Edition

Edited by Tara Walker and Maria Modugno
Designed by Isabelle Arsenault and Kelly Hill
The artwork in this book was rendered in pencils,
watercolor, and ink with digital coloration in Photoshop.
Hand-lettering by Isabelle Arsenault

A Mile End Kids Story

ALBERT'S QUIET QUEST

Words and pictures by
ISABELLE ARSENAULT

Random House 🏠 New York

That's it! QUIET!! For Pete's sake, can't someone just read a book around here or what?!

PURRR...

CLARK ALLEY